IZZY BEAVER GOES

ENVIRONMENTALLY FRIENDLY

By

Mary Gonzalez

Illustrated by
Geoff Cogan

ACKNOWLEDGEMENTS

With special thanks to

Paul Naylor
Silvia Gonzalez
Val Carter
Joan Preston

For all their help in compiling this book

PREFACE

Izzy Beaver and his little friends, Peggy Squirrel, Ron Raccoon, Milly Mole, Harry Hedgehog, Olive Owl, the two little beavers Molly and Betsy, all live on Brockie Field. They have adventures together along with Mickey Ferret, a little ferret who lives down the nearby lane from the field, in a cottage with his owners, the Squire and Lady Jane.

Lady Jane and the Squire befriended Mickey when they found him with a sore paw and lying in the lane. They give Mickey a little red pedal car in which he takes his little friends on the field out and about to the nearby woods and The Three Sisters Recreation area, and Formby beach.

Peggy Squirrel likes to mother everyone, she goes off to the local market every morning to see what she can collect from the stall holders who all make a fuss of her.

She then makes breakfast for all the little creatures. Ron Raccoon likes to be the boss, Harry Hedgehog is a curious little Hedgehog. Izzy Beaver often gets into trouble and has to be rescued by the others, he wears a party hat which he once found on the field hoping it will bring him good luck. Olive Owl likes to fly around the woods at night looking for insects. Farmer Jones' farm is near the field and Daisy the cow who lives there often passes information on about what goes on in the farm and in the woods. The Witch of the Woods lives in a cave in the woods and is not a bad witch, she just gets angry when her spells go wrong, which they nearly always do.

Contents

CHAPTER ONE

It was a bright summer's morning and the

sun shone down on Brockie Field as the little

creatures that lived there began to wake up.

Izzy Beaver was the first to step out of his

little lodge which

was at the side of a

stream which ran

through the field.

'Oh, what a lovely sunny day, I think I'll take a dip in the stream,' he said to himself, and with that he leapt straight into the water and was soon joined by Molly and Betsy, the two little beavers who lived together in their own lodge, next to Izzy's.

All the little creatures living on the field

had, at one time, lived in the nearby woods

before they were chased out by Old Grey

Wolf.

As well as Izzy

Beaver and Molly and

Betsy there was Ron

Raccoon, who had built a little hut in the

centre of the field in which he now lived.

From his doorway he had a good view of the

field, for he liked to keep an eye on what

was going on around him, as well as

organising any events that the little creatures

had. He liked to always be in charge, he was

the bossy one!

Then there was Peggy Squirrel, her

home was in the trunk of the old oak tree.

Peggy liked to mother the little creatures

and, as part of that mothering, she would go

to the market every morning to pick up bits

of fruit, vegetables, nuts, or anything else

which had fallen to the ground from the

stalls, to take back to the field. Peggy had

been doing this for so long that all the stall

holders knew her, and gave her extra treats,

she would then hurry back to the field to lay

the food out for breakfast for everyone to

share.

Olive Owl, the wise one, lived in a nest at

the top of the same tree that Peggy Squirrel

had made her home in. Olive liked to fly

around the field at night making sure that all

was well before flying off to the nearby

church belfry to meet up with her friend,

Barny Bat, who lived in the belfry.

Olive Owl was the one who usually came

to the rescue of Izzy Beaver when he got

into trouble, something that happened quite

often.

Harry Hedgehog lived in a hole at the

bottom of a large tree also on the field. Harry

was a curious little creature, some would say

he was nosey!

Milly Mole lived in tunnels she had dug out for herself under the field.

Milly liked nothing better than tunnelling, and was quite happy just doing that; she was rather timid, and had to be encouraged to go out and about with the other little creatures.

The little creatures had a friend called Mickey Ferret, he lived in a cottage near the field with his owners, Lady Jane, and her husband the Squire.

Lady Jane doted on Mickey and had

bought him a smart, red, pedal car, in which

he took all of his friends from Brockie Field,

out and about the countryside.

On this particular sunny day Peggy

Squirrel was woken up by the loud ringing of

her alarm clock, a clock which she had found

in a ditch and recycled; the little creatures

never let anything go to waste.

She jumped up and peeped out of her

door.

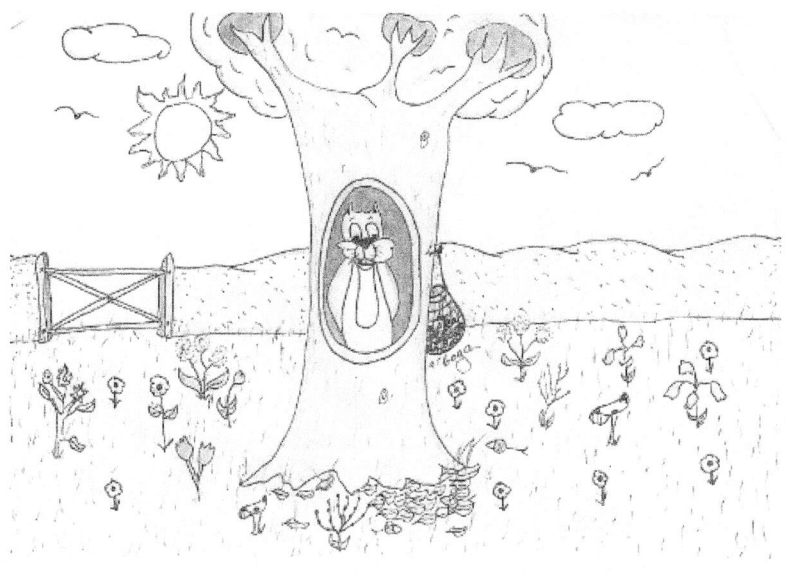

'What a lovely morning,' she said, as she

picked up her basket and skipped off to the

market to see what goodies she could find.

As she went along Peggy could see

sparrows darting in and out of the leafy

hedges that lined the country lanes. The air

was filled with the sweet smell of blossoms

from the hedges and the wild flowers that

grew on each side of the lanes. Bees and

wasps buzzed around and Peggy

remembered how she, and all the other little

creatures had, not so long ago, saved some

bees from the Witch of the Woods.

The witch lived in a cave in the woods.

She was not really a bad witch, it was just

that sometimes she would struggle to get her

spells right and would get herself into quite a

bad temper when they went wrong.

But she never cast a spell on humans.

Once, she had tried to make a small stool

taller, by putting a spell on it, and the stool

had turned into a time machine.

She had still not been able to restore her

stool, tall or short!

The little creatures were very happy with this situation. They kept themselves in the witch's good books because then, she would let them borrow the machine to travel back in time and have the most wonderful adventures.

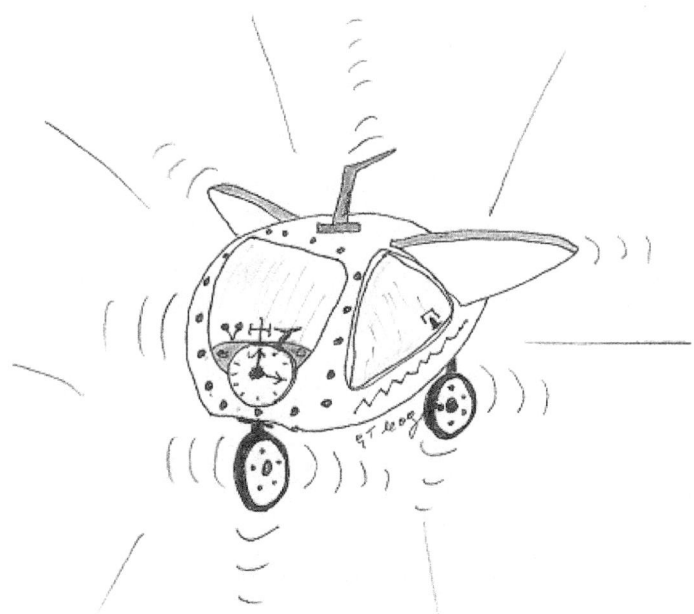

However, there was one time when they had risked upsetting the witch and that was when she had captured some bees.

It turned out that the witch did not like

bees, she was afraid they would sting her.

So, when she found a hive she decided to

put a spell on it and change it into something

more to her liking, however, the little

creatures found out about this.

Now, the little creatures all knew how

important bees are to the planet, gathering

pollen and spreading it around other plants,

and gathering nectar and taking it back to

their hives to make honey. So they hatched

a plan, and had very cleverly outwitted the

witch and were able to rescue the bees.

With her mind still on the bee rescue,

Peggy arrived at the market.

CHAPTER TWO

Arriving at the market Peggy Squirrel found that it was quite busy.

The stalls were set out, displaying their goods for sale.

There was a fish stall and a vegetable stall. A stall selling dairy products such as eggs and cheeses. One was selling cooked ham, sliced meats, and sausage, another was selling tasty homemade jams, cakes and biscuits, and the shoppers were already queuing up to buy, and fill their shopping bags.

The fishmonger caught sight of Peggy and threw her some tit bits of fish, she caught them and put them straight into her basket. 'This will make a tasty treat for Izzy Beaver, Betsy and Molly,' said Peggy, as she wiggled her bushy tail, as a thank you to the fishmonger, who didn't know that's what she meant.

The baker on the cake stall also threw her some bits. He threw her some broken biscuits, and a couple of cakes left over from the day before. 'I'm sure Ron Raccoon will just love these,' thought Peggy. 'He has a bit

of a sweet tooth.'

Then she darted in and out of the stalls,

avoiding the shopper's feet, filling her basket

as she went. She found apple cores,

squashed bananas, grapes, lettuce leaves

and cabbage leaves and some nuts as well,

all of which had fallen from the stalls onto

the ground. Spotting some cloves of garlic

under the greengrocer's table, though she

was not sure what she would use them for,

she nevertheless, quickly scooped them up

and popped them into her basket as well.

When her basket started to feel a little

heavy, she decided to make her way back

home to Brockie Field, walking slowly this

time instead

of skipping.

She was

certain she

had gathered

enough food

for all of her friends, including Mickey Ferret, who often drove onto the field in his little red car to join them for breakfast, even though Lady Jane always made sure he was well fed with the finest ferret food before he left the cottage.

While Peggy Squirrel had been away at the market the little creatures were busy themselves.

Milly Mole kept an old, red, check tablecloth in one of her tunnels. She had found it on the field, where it had been left behind by some picnickers and had kept it to use on their own, home built table.

Milly Mole often collected things that the picnickers left behind, such as spoons and forks, both plastic and metal, and beakers. Plus, paper plates, paper napkins and paper tablecloths.

Some people could be quite thoughtless!

Once she had found a party hat and Izzy Beaver claimed it for himself and always wore it on his head, he thought that it would bring him good luck.

No one knew if Izzy wore the hat when he went to bed though!

As Milly spread the cloth over the table,

Harry Hedgehog appeared, passing her

some worms which he had collected, they

were for Olive Owl, for he knew Olive liked

worms, and he also knew that she would pay

them a short

visit at the

breakfast

table before

flying off to

her nest,

where she

would sleep

the day away after her night's hunting with

Barney Bat.

Izzy Beaver, Molly, Betsy and Ron

Raccoon were busy inspecting the bug hotel

which the little creatures had built.

They had built it some time ago so that

any bugs, spiders, beetles, insects, toads

that happened to find their way into it would

be safe and sound during the winter months,

and they knew that in doing this they would

be helping the environment.

It all came about because one day, on a

visit to the Three Sisters Recreational Area,

they had overheard the Ranger telling some visitors how important it was to look after the wildlife and insects, how they played a vital role in our lives and for the wellbeing of our planet.

He had shown the visitors a scheme in which they had just finished building a series of bug hotels.

And so, the friends had gone home and did as the Ranger, they built their own bug hotel on Brockie Field.

Each 'room' was made of different materials, to suit different 'guests.' Some had straw and sticks in them, others dry leaves and moss, and others had small tufts of sheeps' wool, which the little friends had gathered from where it had become caught on the wire fences surrounding the nearby pastures.

Nothing was left to waste!

The bug hotel kept the insects safe and warm throughout the winter months, and although it was now summer, not all of the residents had been in a hurry to leave.

In one of the 'rooms' a little toad sheltered among the straw and stones.

Suddenly the clanging sound of a bell could be heard all over the field.

Peggy Squirrel was ringing her hand bell

to let everyone

know she was

back, the table

was laden with

the goodies she

had collected

Breakfast was ready!

CHAPTER THREE

The little creatures all tucked into their

breakfast.

Olive Owl was almost falling asleep at the

table, she had been flying around the woods

all night looking for insects with her friend

Barney Bat.

Sadly, they had not managed to catch much because it had rained hard during the night so, though tired, Olive was quite hungry and gratefully tucked into the worms that Harry Hedgehog had collected for her.

Ron Raccoon tucked into the broken biscuits, and Izzy Beaver and Molly and Betsy Beaver tucked into the tasty bits of fish.

Milly Mole munched on a banana, and Harry Hedgehog nibbled at some lettuce leaves. Peggy Squirrel scattered the nuts on the ground for the birds and helped herself before she poured her special, homemade, dandelion juice, into little cups. Peggy had found these cups just lying around on the field, she had picked them up and now kept them in her cupboards, along with plates and many other items that had been carelessly left as litter by uncaring people.

Good for Peggy Squirrel - her motto? Waste not, want not!

Just at that point, Mickey Ferret drove up in his little red car.

He had already had his morning bowl of

ferret food and was full up. He just asked for

a cup of dandelion juice, because he said

that pedalling the car was very thirsty work.

Daisy the Cow wobbled onto the field to

join them. Daisy lived on Farmer Jones' farm

which was next to Brockie Field. She was

the one who told the little creatures about

everything that went on, on the farm, but not

just on the farm, she seemed to be the 'news

reporter' for the surrounding district and woods, too.

The little birds that flew into her cow shed each morning told her all the latest district news, and she overheard all the local gossip from the milkmaids as they chatted away while she was attached to the milking machines in the milking parlour.

'What's new Daisy?' asked the ever-curious Harry Hedgehog.

Daisy usually wanted a mint ball in exchange for any news she would tell. She just loved chewing on a tasty mint ball!

It was Mickey Ferret who supplied Daisy with the mint balls, he always had a pocket full, they were given to him, as he left home each day, by his doting owner Lady Jane.

'I suppose you want a mint ball Daisy, for any information you are about to share with us,' said Mickey Ferret, taking a mint ball out of his pocket in readiness.

'No! I don't want mint balls ever again,' said Daisy, making her mind up.

Everyone stopped eating and looked at Daisy in complete surprise. This was indeed something very unusual, Daisy, not wanting a mint ball. She usually tried to drag her news out while trying to sneak a second mint ball.

'My goodness, are you ill?' asked a shocked Peggy Squirrel.

'No! not at all. The trouble is I have had to change my diet, as Farmer Jones has decided to do everything, he can to help the environment.' 'He is going all out to do his bit to save the planet.'

'What do you mean?' asked Harry Hedgehog, who was by now very interested

'Well, he says that according to the scientists there is something happening to our planet called global warming. Globally warming means that the earth is warming up and this in turn, is causing more flooding, wildfires and extreme weather conditions as well as causing the ice-caps to melt at the North and South Poles.' said Daisy. 'This being the case, we all need to help the environment in any way we can, we should all work together to change things, to stop this global warming. Just think of the poor polar bears.'

'Farmer Jones is having lots of work done on the farm to make it environmentally friendly. But you will be able to see for yourselves when you come to the farm, because, when all the work is completed, he is going to organise an open day.

He is going to invite the public to come and see what he has done, to see and understand how, it will work. They will be able to see how he, Farmer Jones, is doing his part to help save our planet.'

'What has that got to do with you not eating mint balls?' interrupted Harry Hedgehog.

'Well,' said Daisy, a little embarrassed, 'When cows eat the grass, microbes in our stomachs break it down into gas, so when we burp, or trump, but mostly when we burp, we release a gas called methane, and methane, is absolutely not good for the atmosphere,' said Daisy. 'It's not helping the planet at all.'

'It's not good for us either, if we're too close to your bottom,' whispered Izzy chuckling to himself.

'So,' continued Daisy, who hadn't heard Izzy's remark. 'Farmer Jones is putting the herd on a special diet, doing his bit to try to help in stopping what is called, the greenhouse effect.'

'One of the things he is trying is a change of diet for the herd. Giving us more corn grain, and unsaturated fats, which includes whole soya beans and fishmeal, among other things. I've even heard that seaweed may be on the menu. I'm not sure how I feel about that!'

'But surely mint balls are not part of the problem,' said Peggy Squirrel. 'You don't eat that many.'

'I'm taking no chances. We've all got to do our bit you know, so, from now on, no more mint balls for me!' declared Daisy Cow.

'Can you eat garlic?' enquired Peggy Squirrel, wondering if she had found a use for the garlic she had found at the market.

'Yes, garlic is good for me,' said Daisy. 'It seems that garlic will help to keep my gases down, and the smell from them comes through the pores of my skin and helps stop the midges and flies from attacking me. So from now on garlic will be my form of payment for any information given.'

Mickey Ferret picked up one of the cloves of garlic from the table and threw it to Daisy, who promptly caught it, and began to chew as she trotted off, back to the farm having

reported the latest news.

Standing there, watching Daisy go, Izzy

was not too sure about the garlic. He thought

they were going to exchange the smell of

one thing for another.

While at the same time, Peggy made a

mental note for her future shopping lists,

garlic for Daisy Cow.

CHAPTER FOUR

The little creatures finished breakfast and went their separate ways.

Olive Owl flew off to her nest for her daytime sleep. Milly Mole went to do some more tunnelling under the field. Harry Hedgehog went in search of fresh little twigs to make his home cosier and warmer, and Mickey Ferret decided to clean his car.

Izzy Beaver decided to search for tadpoles. Izzy lost his balance on the edge of the stream; he slipped on a plastic bag on the floor. As he fell in, the bag got caught up on Izzy's foot. Very quickly Izzy was struggling to stay on top of the water and found himself unable to swim. 'Help!' cried Izzy, as he began to panic, he had become entangled in a large plastic bag. Two sets of hands grabbed him, and pulled him out of the water.

'One, two, three, heave! we've got him,' shouted a voice.

As the rescuing hands put him down on the ground, Izzy, who had his eyes tightly closed, opened them to see two children, a boy and a girl, standing over him. They quickly unwrapped the plastic bag which Izzy had become entangled in. 'Oh, you poor little beaver,' said the boy.

'Some thoughtless person has thrown this plastic into the stream,' 'Yes,' added the little girl, as she gently stroked Izzy's face. 'There seems to be a lot of other bits of rubbish in there. Look, over there, I can see bottles and cans of pop mixed in with other things. Some people are so thoughtless, not only are they

spoiling pretty places. They are putting

wildlife at danger'. But how are you little

beaver, are you okay now?'

‘Beavers don't talk,’ said the little boy,

smiling to himself at the thought of a beaver

talking. ‘I wish there was something we

could do to stop people throwing rubbish into

the streams and rivers, the seas and even

the oceans. We need to tell our teacher, he

might have some ideas.'

The gentle stroking and quiet whispers

had calmed Izzy Beaver down after his big

fright of nearly drowning.

Seeing that the beaver was ok the children got up and brushed themselves down. 'We'll have to go now, little beaver, or we'll be late for school, so goodbye, and take care of yourself,' chorused the two children as they turned to run off in the direction of their school playground.

As he watched the children hurrying away, Izzy wished he could speak to them, so that he could shout a big thank you to them for rescuing him.

That evening all the little creatures gathered around in the Storytelling Corner.

The Storytelling Corner was their special

place on Brockie Field where they had set

up their homemade benches.

It was the place they gathered together in

the evenings to tell each other what had

happened, or what adventures each had had

during the day.

CHAPTER FIVE

Olive Owl had woken from her daytime sleep and was as eager as ever to join in before going on her nightly hunt with Barney Bat. Barney himself hardly ever came to the field, he was either fast asleep or hunting, he wasn't really much interested in anything else.

Mickey Ferret turned up in his little car and parked it at the edge of the field and went to join the others in the corner.

Peggy Squirrel brought some potatoes

from her store of vegetables to cook in the

fire which Ron Raccoon had made with twigs

and bits of wood, and of which he was in

sole charge of. Ron made sure that all the

little creatures obeyed the safety rules

around the fire.

Izzy Beaver was the first to tell his story and he told his friends how he had been rescued by the children from nearly drowning in the stream.

'Oh dear! Poor you. What a terrible thing to happen to you. I'm so glad that you were saved and are here to tell the tale' said a shocked Molly Beaver.

`We'll have to make the stream a priority and clean it up along with the ditches when we do our usual clean up around here,' said Ron Raccoon.

The little friends regularly went around picking up litter, even though it wasn't theirs.

They cleaned the ditches and streams in order to keep the surrounding countryside safe for the other little creatures and birds living there and to keep it tidy and looking pretty.

It was on those days that, if they found anything useful, they would take it home, clean it up and reuse it.

Things such as Peggy's clock, their tablecloth and cups.

Harry Hedgehog then said, thoughtfully, 'Do you think that we, as a group, are doing enough to help save our planet?'

'Well Harry! We have done some very useful things when you think back. Do you not remember when we saved the Argus Butterfly, who, after losing her home in the wetlands of Manchester, because of a building programme, got herself lost searching far and wide for her favourite food, Hare's-tail grass and Cotton grass.

'Having flown all the way from Manchester she was completely exhausted, remember? We took her on to Astley Moss where there are now peatlands and wetlands growing all the different types of food that Argus Butterflies need.'

'Peatland and wetlands are important, because they help to capture CO2 - that's Carbon Dioxide to you Harry - explained Betsy Beaver, which comes from car exhaust emissions, and smoke which comes out of factory chimneys.' 'That particular Argus Butterfly settled down very well in her new home, along with a hundred other Argus Butterflies which had been released from the zoo.'

'Well remembered Betsy,' congratulated Molly Beaver.

'Yes, I do remember now that you've reminded me, of course I remember. We did help, didn't we?' said Harry.

``We've also helped nature by building a bug hotel on this field,' said Mickey Ferret, who was the one who always provided the tools for any jobs that had to be done, borrowing them from his owner, the Squire.

'That's also true, said Harry Hedgehog, and don't forget, there is still a resident in there, Toad. I don't know what his name is, so I just call him Toad.'

Peggy Squirrel suddenly remembered that on her trip to the market that morning she had seen, and heard, bees and wasps buzzing around the blossoms in the hedgerows and the wild flowers along the ditches. 'Oh, yes,' she said. 'Don't forget that we saved the bees from the Witch of the Woods before she put a spell on them, just because she

didn't like them. I don't think the witch

realised how important they are.'

'Yes, of course, the bees are so important

to humans we must look after them,' said

Harry Hedgehog, wanting to add a little more

to the conversation.

'I also remember when we took a Christmas tree to Formby Beach and planted it there in the sand dunes to help stop the sand from eroding away.' 'The Natterjack Toads that live in the dunes were very pleased to see us,' said Ron Raccoon.

'I remember that on another of our adventures we went to Wales, where we helped the Natterjack Toads to escape to Formby Beach. They were being culled because there were too many of them on the sand dunes in certain areas.' said Harry Hedgehog, shuddering at the thought of the fate of the poor Natterjack Toads.

While his mind was set on toads he thought of the bug hotel resident with no name, and he felt happy that he was safe.

'What is most important,' interrupted Ron, 'Is that we recycle anything of use that we find, I do wish everyone was as thoughtful.'

He was thinking about the plastic and Izzy's narrow escape.

'In the past, he continued, we found railway sleepers and made our table with them.

We reuse any cups and cutlery we find. We once made a go kart out of an old pram and had lots of fun on that.'

'I remember the go-kart in particular, said

Izzy Beaver, it was for one of my birthdays.'

'Supper is ready,' called Peggy Squirrel, putting a stop to the discussion, as Ron Raccoon took the potatoes out of the fire and put them on plates which Peggy held out to him, which she then passed on, one by one, to the friends who were all eagerly awaiting the supper treat of roasted jacket potatoes.

They never got tired of roasted jacket potatoes!

CHAPTER SIX

Everywhere on Brockie Field was quiet.

Everyone was silent, they were busy

eating; but as they ate, the little creatures

had no idea they were being watched.

Breaking the silence of the corner, Izzy

Beaver said "I do wish that I could talk to

humans, I would love to be able to thank

those children who helped me, it is after all

only good manners, apart from the fact that I

am extremely grateful.'

The little creatures could communicate with each other but not with humans, with the exception of the Witch of the Woods.

Sadly, other humans did not think the witch was a human, and in times gone by had been extremely cruel to her ancestors, and to this day she still stays well away from them. Maybe that's why her only friends are the little creatures.

But, no sooner had Izzy expressed his wish, when there was a loud crash, and an even louder screech, and to their surprise they saw the Witch of the Woods lying, sprawled on the ground, with her spell book and broomstick beside her and her hat all

bent and partly drooped over her eyes.

'Oh dear,' said a nervous Milly Mole.

'Where did she come from?'

'She must have been hiding in the oak

tree,' said Ron Racoon. 'I think she's been

spying on us, and she's fallen out of it.'

The witch picked herself up and brushed

herself down, muttering under her breath.

'My poor cat, Trixie, has hurt her paw. She cut it on a piece of broken glass, a bottle someone must have carelessly thrown away in the woods, now she can't ride with me on my broomstick, we have to wait for the wound to heal. I can't balance properly without Trixie sitting on the broomstick with me, I keep falling off.' 'I've done it so many times today, I just don't think I can cope any more,' she cried, rubbing her head and pushing her hat back in place.

'Yes, people should behave more responsibly with their rubbish. They should put things in the correct recycling bins, especially things like glass bottles, ' said Ron Raccoon.

The witch turned to face Izzy Beaver and said, 'Well now Izzy, I wasn't listening, really I wasn't, but as I was in the oak tree, I couldn't help overhearing your conversation about wishing that you could speak to humans,' said the witch, smiling sweetly.

'Yes, you are right about that, I would very much like to be able to thank the school children for helping me, and saving me, but I can't communicate with them,' said Izzy, heaving a sigh.

'I think I can actually help you, if you'll let me,' said the witch, again she smiled sweetly.

'Whoa! Hang on! Wait a minute!' said Ron Raccoon, who was suspicious of the witch's sweet smiles. 'Tell us first what you want from us. Since when have you ever done something for nothing?'

Ron felt it his duty to protect his friends from whoever, or from whatever, might go wrong.

'I would just like you to help clear up the woods,' replied the witch. 'I've noticed that there is so much rubbish, and broken glass lying around lately, I don't know where it all comes from. We need to do a good scavenger hunt, clearing the woods of all the litter. I don't want my poor Trixie getting injured again.'

'We could do that, no problem!' said Ron. 'I don't know where all the rubbish comes from either, my friends and I always pick up any rubbish that we see lying around, we do that because we know it would be helping nature and the environment.'

The others were all in agreement with Ron.

'Now that our side of the bargain is agreed upon, how can you help me to communicate with the children?' asked Izzy.

The witch gave a loud cackle, tapped her nose with her fore finger and winked.

CHAPTER SEVEN

The little creatures stood looking at the witch wondering and worrying, what plan she had up her baggy sleeves.

'I've got my magic wand with me, I can just simply put a spell on you, nothing to it' said the witch reaching into one of her many pockets and pulling out a wand.

'Oh no! Izzy! Don't let her, all her spells go wrong,' wailed a frightened Milly Mole. 'You could end up not being able to talk to us either!'

It was too late, the witch had already

started to chant her spell.

'Fire, bubble,
mixed with tails of dog
and fur of bear,
Give Izzy Beaver a voice
for humans to hear,'

Chanted the witch, waving her wand

around in a very theatrical manner.

Everyone was silent, holding their breath,

waiting for something to happen.

A few seconds passed before Izzy Beaver

started to bark like a dog. He jumped around

and around in circles, barking louder and

louder.

'Oh no! I warned you Izzy. I did warn him,

everyone, but no, you wouldn't listen to me,

you know her spells always go wrong.'
squealed Milly Mole, wringing her paws and
jumping out of Izzy's way.

Izzy continued barking and chasing his tail
in circles.

A confused witch stood watching
scratching her head 'I'm so sorry about that,
a slight hiccup on my part, I'll try again.'
Waving her wand again she began to
chant a second spell.

'A spider's leg,
a cat's whisker,
boil and bubble,
stir with a fork,

and you shall talk,'

Izzy's bark turned into a funny gruff voice,

that surprised his friends.

'Splendid!' said the witch, 'Of course, you

will have noticed that it's not your usual

voice, Izzy, it's a much deeper pitch than

usual. This is so that humans will be able to

hear you when you speak,' she explained.

She then flew away before the little

creatures could ask any questions.

Questions like, how long would the spell last? would he still be able to talk to his friends? would he be able to speak to all humans, or just the children? would Izzy ever be the same again?

CHAPTER EIGHT

The next morning Izzy woke up at his usual time and peeped out of his lodge. He could see Peggy Squirrel hurrying from the field with her basket on her arm, on her way to the market. The other little creatures gathered together to do what they usually did, they set the table ready for Peggy's return.

'I must go and see if I can find those kind children and thank them for saving me from the plastic in the stream,' said Izzy. '

Without telling the others where he was

going Izzy ran off to the school just

next to the field. 'Maybe the children who

saved me go to this school,' he told himself,

as he arrived at the school gates, keeping a

good look out so he didn't bump into any

parents. Looking through the railings he

could see the children coming out of the

school into the playground.

However, there were so many that Izzy did not recognize anyone. He stood there, continuing to peep through the railings, watching the children running around the playground playing tag, it made him dizzy watching them.

Dizzy Izzy, he thought, and smiled to

himself, he thought this could be a good game he could show his friends back home to all play together.

'This is going to be mission impossible,' and was just about to give up and leave when the two children saw him.

'Oh, look Jack, there's the beaver we saved from the water,' said the little girl excitedly. 'You are so right, Emily, I would recognise that party hat anywhere.'

Running over to Izzy the children said

'Hello little beaver, you look good today after that scary accident you had yesterday,' Trying to stroke Izzy through the school railings, Izzy replied 'finally I've found you, I wanted to thank you for saving me yesterday, my name is Izzy Beaver,' he said, in his new, low-pitched voice.

The children looked at Izzy in amazement. 'Did you hear that, Jack, I don't believe it! I heard him speak, did you?' said an amazed Emily.

'Izzy looked just as amazed as the children to hear his new voice. He tried it again 'Did you mean it yesterday when you said you wondered how you could help the

countryside and keep it tidy? If so, I have

some ideas you could share with your

teacher and see if you could help in any

way.' Jack and Emily still in shock from a

talking beaver stood at their school gates,

got closer to Izzy to hear how they could

help.

'Firstly, you could help by letting people

know how dangerous it is for the wildlife if

they throw things carelessly onto the streets

or roads, in ditches, fields, streams and

rivers, especially plastic, look what

happened to me, and we must especially

keep plastic out of the seas. Do you know how many sea creatures, dolphins, whales and turtles and such like, die from getting bits of plastic stuck in their tummies?'

'Another very easy thing you can do is, if you have any clothes that you don't use, or that you may have grown out of, if you don't pass them on to your brothers or sisters, you could put them in the recycle bin over there,' said Izzy pointing to a big red bin where a lady had just dropped in a rather large parcel. 'And why not build a bug hotel in your garden, in fact you could build one on the spare land at the back of your school, if your teacher would allow it. There are lots of

little bugs there that have lost their homes

because a major road has been built along

the edge of it.'

'Or you could plant a tree in your garden,

on the other hand, if your garden is too

small, you could plant shrubs in containers.

If you have a larger garden ask your parents,

when they mow the lawn to leave a clump of

uncut grass, and scatter a mixture of wild

flower seeds, such as poppies, dandelions

and buttercups. This will make a mini

meadow in your own back garden.

When the seeds become flowers they will

provide nectar for the bees, and butterflies,

and the taller grass will provide homes for all

sorts of little creatures that we very rarely

see because they hide away. So, then you

can study them.'

'When Autumn comes the seed heads

from the flowers provide another kind of food

for the wildlife. Then, when the flowers have

gone completely, the grass can be mown so

that it doesn't become too overgrown and

unmanageable.'

'It will all be good for the environment and will certainly help nature which is a very good thing, for we must all do whatever we can.' said Izzy. 'You must tell your teacher all that I have said, it's very important.'

Izzy's voice started sounding funny as it squeaked and a bark slipped out before slowly returning to his own voice.

The school bell rang for everyone to go into school.

Izzy jumped up and down excitedly that he had been able to tell the children his important message and waved them into school before he raced back to his friends to tell them all he had his voice back.

He now felt that he owed the witch a favour, but what would it be? What could he do for her? She did mention something about tidying up around and about, but the little creatures did that anyway.

He turned the thoughts over in his head as he raced back to Brockie Field.

He wasn't going to miss breakfast, his early morning mini-adventure had left him quite hungry.

He was so hungry he felt as though he could eat Mickey's ferret food and enjoy it!

CHAPTER NINE

Jack and Emily couldn't wait to tell their teacher Mr. Gray and their class about how they saved a beaver and his message to share with them all. Their teacher stroked his beard most thoughtfully. Listening to their story before he added 'Well Jack, Emily you certainly have been busy, there is no doubt that you have vivid imaginations, but I do know that you're not in the habit of making things up. I'm not sure about talking beavers but what great ideas and valuable information you have. Strangely enough our next lesson this morning is about climate

change, so jumping straight in now you have

started us off,' he said.

'Attention class! Today we will talk about

carbon footprints.'

The atmosphere is a protective layer

surrounding the earth, and has carbon

dioxide and other gases in it. It acts as a blanket, keeping the earth warm, just at the right temperature for life It is made up of different gases, we call these the 'Greenhouse gases,' because they act like a greenhouse keeping our planet warm.

'What is a carbon footprint?' asked one of the children.

'A carbon footprint,' Mr. Grey began, 'Is the total amount of greenhouse gases, which include Carbon Dioxide and Methane, caused by what we do as individual human beings, like burning fuel flying aeroplanes

running machinery in factories, running our

cars, which is

slowly making

the blanket, the

protective layer

protecting us from the heat and rays of the

sun, thicker, causing the temperatures to

rise ever so slightly.' 'This is called Global

Warming, and will obviously change the

climate, as we know it, on planet Earth.'

'This, in its turn will begin to melt the ice-

caps at the two Poles, as well as causing all

sorts of natural disasters such as forest fires,

tornadoes, hurricanes and exceptionally high tides causing flooding, and crazy weather patterns.

'To work towards saving the planet, we must all do our bit.' We can help to reduce our 'carbon footprint' by reducing how much energy we use, using our cars less, and walking or cycling more, switching off lights and electrical items when we are not using them etc, or looking for other ways to create energy, (renewables.)

'We have to leave it to governments to pass laws for the large industrial manufacturers, airline companies, and transport companies etc., but we, making

small changes in our lives, can play our part.'

We should turn the lights off when we

leave a room, so saving electricity.

'Such as - when we clean our teeth, we

shouldn't just let the water run: turn the tap

off while you brush.'

'When you take a shower make it a short

one, you only want to wash the day's dust off

you; don't stay in there pretending the shower head is part of a karaoke.'

The children laughed!

'If you're allowed to make a cup of tea, only put as much water in the kettle that is needed, or tell the person making it.'

'There we have just three easy ways to save water, plus two ways of saving electricity.'

'Which two are saving electricity as well as water?' he asked the class. 'Please write the answers in your notebooks, and remember that water is a valuable resource it takes a lot of energy to clean water so that we can drink it. Mr Grey continued, 'In the school canteen Try not to take more food for your plate than you can eat. Try not to waste food as it takes a lot of energy to get the food from the fields to your plate.

When you go shopping with your mum don't ask her to buy something in particular for you and then don't eat it.

Make sure that when you raid the refrigerator, or the fruit bowl, the food you take, you eat. No half eaten, or chewed up bits thrown away.

And there we have three simple ways to avoid food wastage. But, if there are any chewed up bits then recycle them; scrap food, apple cores, banana skins, orange peel, etc., etc., I won't go on,' he said. 'Either put them in compost bins or your waste food caddy.'

'When there is no one in the room, turn the lights off.'

'When you've finished with your computer or gadgets, turn them off rather than on standby so you are not using any electricity while you are not playing on them.'

'The same goes for your parents with their, kettle, microwave or toaster.'

'Those are little ways to save electricity, and money.'

'If you haven't already got one in your garden at home, perhaps you could persuade your dad to leave space among the flowers for a vegetable patch.' 'Or, if you have a slightly shady corner you could help to make a compost bin, or a bug hotel.' 'Now these are two things that we shall be making to put on the school field, and I also hope that the headmaster will allow us to plant a small vegetable garden, with maybe carrots and potatoes, and we can grow tomatoes in containers. We can plant trees

and flowers, plants are like sponges which

soak up the carbon dioxide and locks it

away. The food that we grown will be put on

our plates on the dinner table.

'So, in time, we shall be needing

volunteers to water and to weed the patch. I

shall be explaining why these projects are

good projects, in our carbon footprint

lessons over the next few weeks, when we

shall look at other ways of reducing our

carbon footprint - as we shall call them. See how many suggestions you can come up with, or things that your family is already doing.'

'Now, your homework for the weekend children will be easy. I want you to collect, for our compost bin project, any bits of twigs, tree bark, dry leaves, moss, cardboard, bits of straw. If you used to have a pet and still have some dried pet food, bring that. You can even bring eggshells and your mums' used teabags, plus, would you believe, sweepings from the floor after you boys have had your hair cut at the barbers, or hair salons, in the case of the young ladies in the class. All good stuff for the compost bin.

'And if there are any broken terracotta plant pots lying around your dad's shed, ask him if we can have them, to go towards making our bug hotel.' 'I will call and collect them, if necessary.'

'I have just invented a class motto,' he said, smiling, 'and that motto is - 'Protecting our planet starts with me!'

'Remember, we need to take tiny steps everyone, tiny steps. If everyone in the world took some tiny steps towards reducing their own carbon footprint, then our planet would breathe a great sigh of relief.

Now, good morning children. Off you go!' he said as he finally dismissed them for their dinner break.

The children all laughed as they filed out, chorusing, 'Good morning, Mr. Grey!'

While Mr Grey was instructing his class about carbon footprints and climate change, Peggy Squirrel had returned from the market, and all the little creatures on Brockie Field were happily tucking into their extremely late breakfast.

Mickey Ferret had joined them, and when Izzy told them all about what he had said that very morning to Jack and Emily, Mickey said, 'Lady Jane and the Squire have done something really good to help the environment, guess what it is?' 'They've replaced their petrol car for an electric one, their little bit to help stop polluting the atmosphere, no exhaust emissions'.

'And, as well as that, this morning, Lady Jane only gave me a very short, swift shower, in order not to waste water. I was very happy with that, I can tell you' said Mickey. 'As you all know, I don't particularly like water.'

Then Ron Racoon, laughed out loud, as he stood up at the table and said, 'If an electric car is better for the environment than

a petrol or diesel car, then your car, Micky

Ferret, must be super friendly; because you

only use pedal power!' And all the little

friends joined in laughing, saying, 'Well done

Mickey, you are an environmentally friendly

ferret and you didn't know it.'

CHAPTER TEN

When all the little creatures had finished their breakfast Olive Owl flew away to have her daytime sleep. She had spent the night, as usual, flying around the woods with Barney Bat, and was quite worn out. The others decided to go for a trip out to the Three Sisters Recreational Area, which was not too far from Brockie Field. 'Sort yourselves out, who's riding in the car, I've attached the trailer today, the trailer and all jump in.' called out a cheerful Mickey.

Everyone followed Mickey into the vehicles

and he pedalled away, off the field and away

down the country lane.

When they arrived at the Three Sisters,

they were just in time to see one of the

Rangers feeding the geese and ducks on the

lake. While another one was just setting off

on one of his guided tours around the

grounds.

He had quite a lot of people following him,

all listening to his talks on nature and the

wildlife which lived at Three Sisters.

The little friends went to the play area and

played leapfrog, one of their usual games,

but Harry Hedgehog could not join in this

particular game as his legs were far too

short. Instead, he just wandered around

watching children enjoying themselves on

the swings and slides.

He stood and watched men fishing by the

sides of the lake, but, whatever fish they

caught they always, very gently, slid it back into the water.

Coming towards the end of their game of leapfrog, drops of rain started to fall down.

''We need to hurry and get back home,' warned Ron Raccoon. 'I think there could be a very bad storm on the way.'

Hurriedly, they all climbed back into the car and trailer, and Mickey peddled away as fast as he could, heading home.

A biting, cold wind sprang up and blew the car from side to side as Mickey struggled to drive through the strong wind.

Just a few hours ago it had been sunny and warm, now it was more like a winter's day. The sky had turned dark and hailstones started to rain down, bouncing off the car

and hitting the little creatures.

'Ouch! Ouch,' cried the three beavers, who

had chosen to sit in the trailer.

'This unpredictable weather is all due to

climate change,' said Ron. `We have storms

in summer, but what about all these

hailstones? Where did they come from? This

is all part of the reason why we need to do

our bit in helping the environment.'

The wind became stronger and stronger

and the rainwater was flooding the country

roads, and there was nowhere for the little

creatures to take shelter in the open

countryside. However, they soon came to

the woods and Mickey Ferret said, 'Let's ask

the Witch of the Woods if we can shelter in her cave as the storm seems to be getting worse.'

The little creatures all agreed, anything to get out of the terrible downpour. Their furs were soaking wet through, they looked so bedraggled, and poor Betsy and Molly Beaver began to sneeze. 'Oh my, I think we will all catch colds if we don't find a warm shelter and dry off soon," said Molly to Betsy.

CHAPTER ELEVEN

Mickey Ferret drove carefully, weaving in and out of the trees, the raindrops bouncing off his nose, but soon they arrived at the cave entrance. They could see smoke coming from the roof of the cave, so they knew that the witch was at home. They hovered in the entrance, peeping inside. They could see the witch, she was busy stirring the contents of a huge cauldron,

which was hanging from a hook, dangling

over the fire.

The cave looked the same as it usually

did, with photos of the witch's ancestors

displayed on one of the walls. Spiders' webs

hung down, like dusty net curtains, from the

ceiling. Her broomstick stood in the corner,

next to the time machine, and Trixie the cat

was curled up on a cushion on a ledge at the far end of the cave.

Poor Trixie, she was nursing her sore paw.

There were string bags full of snails, and ropes of garlic bulbs hanging from nails on the wall opposite her ancestor's photo gallery. The table, in the centre of the cave, was already set with bowls and spoons, and rickety old chairs had been placed around it, just as though the witch had been expecting visitors.

Suddenly, as though she had eyes in the back of her head, she spun around and faced them, pointed her scrawny finger and

cackled.

'I knew you were coming. A magpie flew

in a short while ago and told me you were on

your way. What were you thinking of going

out and about in this weather?'

'It was sunny when we set out,' said Ron

Racoon, defensively.

'That's true! You are quite correct, Mr. Racoon,' she said. 'It was a lovely sunny day earlier on, all that rain and hailstone seemed to come from nowhere. But never mind, come in and warm yourselves by the fire and dry your fur before you all catch a chill; then you can sit yourselves down and have some of this soup that I have simmering over the fire.'

The little creatures had never seen the

witch in such a good mood, but they were

still wary, because they also knew how her

moods could change in an instant.

When the little creatures had dried

themselves, and without any further

prompting, they all sat down on the rickety

chairs and tucked into the soup, and garlic

bread, which the witch had piled onto a plate

in the middle of the table.

When they had finished, she said, 'Now

you owe me a favour.'

'I knew it!' said Izzy Beaver to Ron Racoon. 'I knew she would want something in return. She never does anything for nothing.'

'Keep calm, Izzy,' said Ron, 'We knew she would want something in return, she always does, so that's no surprise is it?'

'I am fed up,' the witch continued, ignoring Izzy and Ron's comments, 'with my cave being flooded whenever there are heavy rains, and it seems that there is another storm forecast.

'Oh yes, we brushed all the water out for you when you were flooded out a few weeks ago,' said Harry Hedgehog who remembered everything,' The witch indeed remembered how her cave had been flooded.

'I could do with some sandbags being placed in the entrance to my cave to keep the water out.' 'Now, I happen to know, from

the same magpie that told me about your arrival, that Farmer Jones has spare sandbags in his utility shed. So, that's how

you can repay me, bring two of Farmer

Jones' sandbags and place them at the

entrance of my cave.' 'Now, that isn't much

to ask, is it, after my generous hospitality

towards you all? And, Oh Yes! I will want

you to return them when I'm finished with

them,' she ended, and blew her nose hard,

hoping that she hadn't caught a chill.

The little creatures were reluctant to go on

a mission of any kind, and besides,

sandbags were heavy objects, weren't they?

Then Peggy Squirrel said, 'Look, the rain

has stopped, and we would be doing a good

turn. After all, Izzy, you already owe the witch a favour. The farmer will have plenty of sandbags and we will be saving the witch's cave from being flooded, and everyone should do a good turn whenever they can.

The little creatures didn't realise that Peggy Squirrel had another reason for helping the witch and keeping her sweet. She had seen the ropes of garlic hanging on the wall and hoped the witch would let her have a couple of bulbs to store away for bribing Daisy Cow now that she did not want any more mint balls for news and information.

So, it was agreed, that after they had a

good feast and the fact that everyone should

help each other, when possible, Ron

Raccoon, Mickey Ferret and Izzy Beaver set

off in the car to the farm leaving the others

behind to entertain the witch.

A nervous Milly Mole was not too happy

about having to wait in the cave, she was

worried in case the witch lost her temper and put a spell on her, but fortunately the witch stayed in her happy mood and she entertained them. She gathered them together around the fire and told them stories about when she was a young girl.

Milly found it difficult to imagine that the witch had ever been young.

Gradually, it became quite dark in the cave and the flames from the fire was the only lighting they had. As they moved about, the little creature's shadows were thrown onto the walls of the cave. When they saw this they began to laugh and made 'shadow animal heads,' with their paws, then they jumped up and down and from side to side. They became quite dizzy from twirling around, making their shadows dance.

Milly Mole, however, was still greatly relieved when Izzy, Ron, and Mickey arrived back with two sandbags in the trailer.

Ron Raccoon explained that he had found out that the sandbags on Farmer Jones' farm were for anyone in the community who needed them, so, there would be no need to return them.

Quickly, they put the sandbags one on top of the other to form a sort of small embankment at the cave's entrance, and

hoped that this would stop the cave from

flooding.

The witch was really pleased and

promised them all a trip in her time machine,

whenever they wanted to.

A promise that the little friends would all

look forward to her keeping!

At last, all tired out, but dry and well fed,

and feeling good because they had been

able to do a good turn for someone; and

Peggy more so than her friends, because

the witch had allowed her to take a whole

rope of garlic bulbs because she had

encouraged the little creatures to fetch the

sandbags. As they made their way back to

their homes, they were all concerned in case

Brockie Field would be flooded.

Thankfully, when they arrived, they were

very relieved to see that all was well,

although the stream was flowing a little

faster.

CHAPTER TWELVE

About a week later, all storms had passed, the sun was out again and the weather was dry with just a light breeze.

The little creatures were just finishing their breakfast, when Mickey Ferret arrived on the field. 'You're later than usual this morning Mickey, what have you been doing?' asked Harry Hedgehog, curious as usual.

'The Squire and Lady Jane were late today putting out my ferret food because they were both busy getting ready for the Open Day at Farmer Jones' farm, which just so happens to be today,' he told them. 'I heard Lady Jane saying that the children from the school, next to our field, are going to be there as well, with their teacher, Mr Grey.'

'The children in his class have been creating a vegetable patch, as well as making a small meadow on part of the playing field where they will scatter wildflower seeds.' 'They're making their own compost bins, and have finished making a bug hotel, and in doing all this they earned lots of house points for themselves and so, as a special treat, they are going to the open day.'

'Oh, I'm so glad that the witch put that spell on me and I was able to talk to Emily and Jack,' said Izzy Beaver. 'I'm even more pleased that they listened to me and did what I suggested.'

'You did a good job there Izzy, well done!' said Peggy Squirrel.

Just then the little creatures could see lots of people, plus all the children from Mr Grey's class, led by Mr Grey himself, walking along the lane towards the farm.

'Why don't we go to the farm as well and see what is going on?' said Harry Hedgehog. Everyone agreed that it was a good idea and they all set off for Farmer Jones' farm.

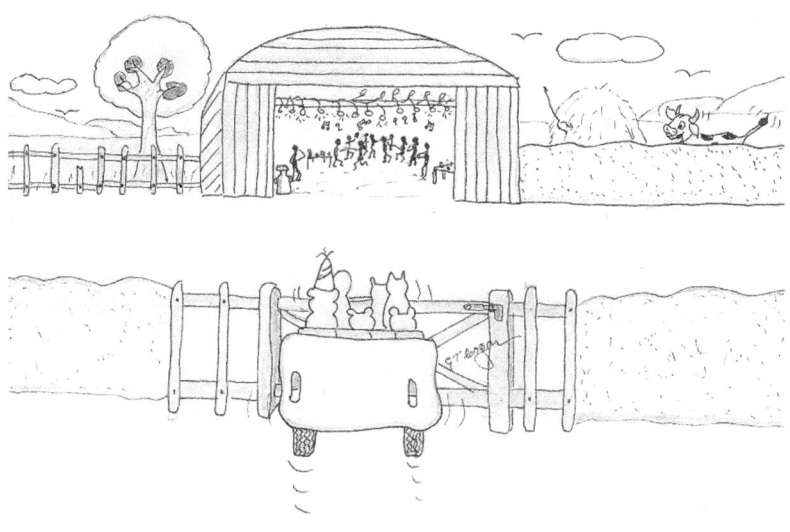

When they arrived, the farm was buzzing with excitement. Everyone was awaiting the arrival of some honoured guests.

A brass band which was playing quietly,

just outside the refreshment tent, suddenly

broke into a loud fanfare as an electrically

driven limousine drove onto the farmyard

and made its way to park next to the farm

cottage.

When it had come to a stop, out stepped

the Lord Mayor and the Lady Mayoress.

As they walked towards Farmer and Mrs Jones, their chauffeur plugged the car into a power point near the back door of the cottage.

The honoured guests had every intention of staying and joining in the day's festivities, and it wouldn't do for the battery of the mayoral limousine to be flat for the journey home.

All the visitors clapped as the Lord Mayor and Lady Mayoress shook hands with Farmer Jones and his wife as Farmer Jones proudly invited them, and all the other people who had gathered around, to follow him for a guided tour of his farm.

Firstly, he pointed out the solar panels he had installed on the cottage roof and on the roof of the stable block. He explained that solar panels gather energy from the sun's rays to provide the farm cottage and stables with enough electricity for all their needs, and what they didn't need could be stored.

One of the children piped up, 'What happens in the winter when there is no sunshine?'

'Even though you cannot see the sun, it is still there, or we wouldn't have daylight,' put in Mr Grey.

'But as well as solar panels I have also had wind turbines installed in my fields and they can produce electricity as well.' 'You see, when the wind blows the arms of the turbines are turned, just like a windmill, although the 'sails' on the turbines and the windmills are very different from each other, as you can see,' said Farmer Jones, as he led them away towards his orchards.

The sight of the turbine 'sails' turning in the wind, and the mention of windmills made

Izzy Beaver feel rather queasy. He was

remembering their visit to Parbold, when he

had found himself in trouble, as usual, and

had to be rescued, as usual, from clinging to

the 'sails' of the windmill as he was blown

around and around by the wind.

Izzy would not make the same mistake

again.

When the crowd arrived at the orchards,

they found agriculture students busy at work

extending them. They were planting pear

and damson trees to grow alongside the

apple trees already growing there, all of

which the farmer had bought in London on

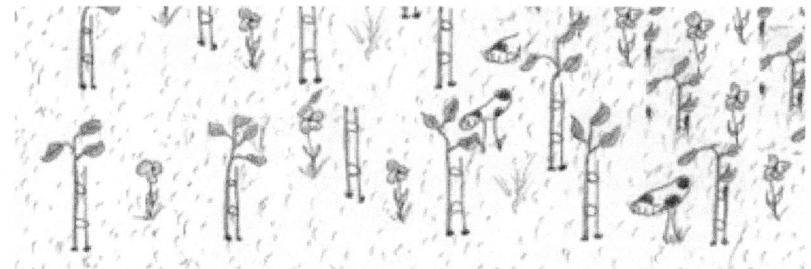

visits to Kew Gardens.

Farmer Jones then walked the visitors past

a small lake on the way to the bottom

meadow where the sheep shearing sheds

were.

He stopped at the lake where Tommy

Tinker was painting a sign 'DO NOT FEED

THE DUCKS.'

'When people feed the ducks white bread

it fills them up and they don't eat their

 meals,' said Tommy

putting a final stroke

to the sign.

'This lake,' said the

farmer, 'Hasn't always been here, but I'll let

Tommy Tinker tell you the story behind it.'

'Well,' began Tommy, feeling quite

important.

'During World War Two, I was just a young lad you understand, helping out on the farm to earn a few pennies, and this Farmer Jones and I were schoolmates. Food was in short supply because of the war and everyone had to do the best they could, by growing as much as they could, wherever they could, and so, Farmer Jones Senior had the original lake filled in and grew extra vegetables for - the War Effort - as it was called.'

'Everyone forgot about the lake.'

'Then, by the time Farmer Jones Junior took over, everyone was beginning to talk of helping the environment, nature and the

ozone layer, so he had some students from

the Agricultural College help him to dig out

the land, which was by that time just part of

the field, and refill it with water.'

'So, as you can see, the lake is flourishing

with wildlife, we have dragonflies, mayflies,

butterflies, you name the flies, we've got

them.' 'We have pond skippers, frogs and

newts.'

'We also have ducks - Mallards, Grebe

and Coots, plus one or two Mute swans

which stay with us all year round. Added to

that, in winter the lake can be a stopping of

point for winter visitors, such as Whooper

Swans on their way from their summer

homes in Iceland, and the Berwick Swans

from their homes in Arctic Russia, to rest for

a while on their way to the wetlands and

nature reserves to meet up with swan

relatives, such as the Canada Geese who

stay here all year round, and, more

importantly for their 'winter holidays' as you

might say.' 'For it's much warmer here than

in their homelands during the winter months.'

When Tommy Tinker had finished his tale

the Lord Mayor thanked him very much for

 his

explanation,

and Tommy

thanked the

crowd for listening.

Farmer Jones then moved his guests on towards the shearing sheds.

When they got there, they saw one of the shepherds, Betty Bobbins, wrapping the sheared wool into bales to be sent on to the mills in order to be processed into loft insulation. According to her, using the processed sheep's wool for insulation was a much better, and more environmentally friendly product to insulate with than the materials which were previously used, and still in use. She said it was just as efficient in preventing heat escaping through the walls and roofs of people's homes, thus helping them to save energy, as well as money on their electricity bills.

'Saving money, saving energy, as well as helping to save the planet,' said Betty. 'Can't do better than that!'

When Farmer Jones had finished the tour of his environmentally friendly installations, the people went to stroll around the stalls and the children went to play on the swing-boats, the carousel, helter skelter and a

bouncy castle, which Farmer Jones had

hired and set up in his meadow.

All the fun of the fair with none of the

diesel pollution to go with it, none of these

rides needed fuel to run them.

There were quite a few stalls scattered around the farm with a variety of farm, and locally made craft products for sale.

Homemade produce such as honey, which Farmer Jones got from his own beehives, butter and cheeses made by Mrs Farmer Jones, and delicious fruit pies made by Lady Jane, not forgetting Mrs. Tinker's scones which were served in the refreshment tent with lashings of fresh cream and homemade strawberry jam. There were milkshakes, and the creamiest ice-cream, all made in the farm's dairy. What could be fresher?

There were straw dollies and straw hats for sale and straw baskets, too.

One customer, while buying a pie from Lady Jane, asked her where she had bought her lovely dress, and Lady Jane told her that instead of buying new dresses she was remodelling old ones already in her wardrobe. 'I make do and mend,' she said. 'My small contribution towards saving our planet. When you buy something new it uses electricity to make the item, then there is the fuel it takes to get it delivered to you, it might be made in a different country and has to be driven to the aircraft or ship and then when it arrives in the country it takes even more fuel to get it to all the different depots before it is finally delivered to you. So, if you went to a local charity shop or adapted your old clothes or shared your used clothes with your friends when you have finished with them, then this would save a lot of unnecessary energy being used up for the sake of having another new item'.

'That, as well as saving me quite a bit of money on designer clothes, and trips to London,' said the Squire, overhearing the conversation as he walked past.

As the tour of the farm was now over the Lord Mayor and his Lady made their way to a small platform which had been set up with a microphone.

On reaching the microphone he called for everyone's attention, then, on behalf of himself and his wife, he thanked Farmer and Mrs Jones for their hospitality and most informative tour of the farm, he then announced to the people gathered around, the reason for his being there.

He was at the farm, he said, to give an award to Farmer Jones and his wife and all his staff for their excellent work installing all the new environmentally friendly schemes on the farm. Because Farmer Jones was using renewable energy there was no need to burn fuel. He also thanked the school and all the children for all their recent hard work and new projects they were starting on improving their environment at their school and surrounding areas to help reduce their carbon footprint.

They then asked Farmer and Mrs Jones and all the farm staff, plus Lady Jane and the Squire, to join them in being photographed for the local newspaper.

Farmer Jones was so pleased, he held the trophy, which the Mayoress had presented him with, high and proudly in the air for everyone to see; all the visitors clapped and cheered. Another good photo for the paper!

Izzy Beaver made sure he'd managed to

sneak onto at least one of the photographs,

for he liked nothing more than attracting

attention; but heaven knows what people

would think when they saw a beaver in a

party hat in the photograph with the Lord

Mayor and the Lady Mayoress, taken at the

now - very environmentally friendly farm!

A good time had been enjoyed by all and

as the afternoon faded away, the farmer had

arranged for a small firework display, which

brought lots of 'oohs' and 'aahs' from the

children still present.

A dance followed in the barn, with food

and refreshments for everyone.

Izzy also made sure that all the little

creatures attended the barn dance, where

they gathered together, well away from the feet of the dancers.

Some of the school children had returned with their parents for the barn dance. How surprised they were when they caught sight of the little creatures all gathered together in a corner nibbling on bits of food that a kind lady had put down for them.

One of the children said to Emily, 'Look, I think one of those animals is a beaver, I've never seen a beaver before. Have you?'

'Yes,' said Emily. 'So have,' I said Jack.

'Ah! Go on, I don't believe either of you,' said the boy.

Neither had Mr. Grey, but he hadn't told them.

Lady Jane made sure there was plenty of fruit, nuts, salad leaves, and anything else she thought that Mickey, and his friends,

would like to eat, just within reach of their eager paws.

From their vantage point the little

creatures caught sight of the Witch of the

Woods flitting into the barn and helping

herself to a plate of cakes, before quickly

flitting out again before anyone saw her, or

so she thought.

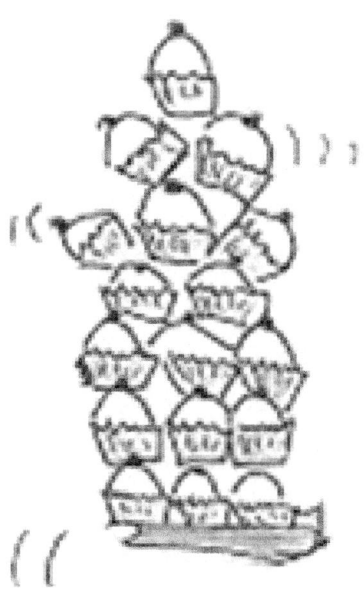

No doubt the magpie had told her of the occasion and she did not want to miss out.

But she was spotted; not only by the now wide-eyed and unbelieving children, but by Lady Jane herself.

'My dear,' she said, turning to the Squire, 'Who is that woman that comes into every barn dance that Farmer Jones has?'

Nothing escaped her notice!

'Oh, no doubt it will be one of the friends of Mickey Ferret,' replied her husband. 'You know, my dear, I believe that Mickey Ferret and his friends get up to all sorts of things that we know nothing about.'

'I agree,' said Lady Jane. 'Who knows, maybe one day we'll find out exactly what it is that they do get up to, but, until then,' Lady Jane stopped and suddenly snatched her breath. 'Well, did you see that, my dear? I could swear that Mickey Ferret just winked at us.'

THE END.

IZZY BEAVER BOOKS

The Adventures of Izzy Beaver and his Friends.
Izzy Beaver goes Go-karting.
Izzy Beaver goes to Sea.
Izzy Beaver and the Metal Detector.
Izzy Beaver and the Hot Air Balloon.
Izzy Beaver goes to the Zoo.
Izzy Beaver goes to the Moon.
Izzy Beaver and the Time Machine.
Izzy Beaver and the Bumble Bee.
Izzy Beaver and the Brown Hare.
Izzy Beaver and the Easter Egg Hunt.
Izzy Beaver and the Halloween Party.
Izzy Beaver and the Bug Hotel.
Izzy Beaver and the Natterjack Toads.
Izzy Beaver and the Truffles.
Izzy Beaver and the Ice Cream Parlour.
Izzy Beaver and the Secret Door.
Izzy Beaver and the Ant Eater.
Izzy Beaver and the Ark.
Izzy Beaver and the Pot of Gold.
Izzy Beaver goes Backpacking.
Izzy Beaver goes to London.
Izzy Beaver Activities Collection.
Izzy Beaver and the Medieval Castle.
Izzy Beaver and the Woodcutter.
Izzy Beaver goes to the Caribbean.
Izzy Beaver and the Railway Sleepers.
Izzy Beaver and the Christmas Tree.
Izzy Beaver and Santa Claus.
Izzy Beaver and the Loch Ness Monster.

www.facebook.com/gonzalezstories

www.izzybeaver.com

Printed in Great Britain
by Amazon

48800558R00096